This book has been donated to
The Concord Library in the honor of

Karen Mitchoff

this 4th day of _Nov_, 201 6 _[signature]_
President

ROTARY
SERVING
HUMANITY

Rotary
Club of Concord

FOR LUKE MICHAEL WILMER

First published as Herman's Holiday in Great Britain in August 2015
by Bloomsbury Publishing Plc
Published in the United States of America in April 2016
by Bloomsbury Children's Books

Bloomsbury is a registered trademark of Bloomsbury Publishing Plc

For information about permission to reproduce selections from this book,
write to Permissions, Bloomsbury Children's Books,
1385 Broadway, New York, New York 10018

Bloomsbury books may be purchased for business
or promotional use. For information on bulk
purchases please contact Macmillan Corporate
and Premium Sales Department at
specialmarkets@macmillan.com

Library of Congress Cataloging-in-Publication Data
available upon request
ISBN 978-1-61963-990-4 (hardcover)

Printed in China by Leo Paper Products, Heshan, Guangdong
2 4 6 8 10 9 7 5 3 1

All papers used by Bloomsbury Publishing, Inc., are natural, recyclable
products made from wood grown in well-managed forests. The manufacturing
processes conform to the environmental regulations of the country of origin.

The day was warm and smelled of summer.
Herman and Henry were busy
planning their vacation.

There were SO MANY
exciting places to go.

But all the best places cost SO MUCH money.

Far too much for Herman and Henry.

It was looking like they'd be staying at home this year. And Henry didn't like *that* one little bit.

Herman hated to see his best friend upset . . .

. . . so he set out to find
a vacation they could afford.

A short while later, Herman had everything
they could possibly need for a fun-packed break.

He was SO excited—after all, EVERYBODY loves camping!

Still, it was all
booked now.

By lunchtime, they had each packed a few
essentials and were ready to go.

As they set off, Herman felt ready for anything.

Henry, on the other hand,
just felt like going home.

Within five minutes of arriving at the
campsite, Herman's tent was up and
the marshmallows were toasting.

But Henry did NOT find
camping quite so easy.

That night, Henry didn't sleep very well.

HOOT!

He just couldn't get comfy. To be perfectly honest,
he was a teeny bit scared.

And that was BEFORE his tent collapsed!

The next morning Herman took Henry into
town to buy some postcards.

But they each wrote
VERY different things . . .

Henry TRIED to enjoy his vacation—
but nothing seemed to be working out for him.

Herman got the impression that his friend wasn't having a particularly great time.

So the next day,
Herman didn't just
write one postcard . . .

he wrote TONS!

Before long, strange packages began to arrive for Herman.

It was all VERY mysterious.

That night, Herman waited until
his friend fell asleep . . .

and he put his plan into action!

By the time the sun rose,
the campsite had been
transformed.

Henry couldn't believe

his eyes!

The two friends spent the rest of their time doing all the things that make a GREAT vacation.

Everything was just perfect!

But despite everything that he had built, Herman refused to abandon his tent.

Good night!

GOOD NIGHT

HOTEL HE

After all, this WAS a camping trip.